CFB GREENWOOD
BASE LIBRARY REGULATIONS

THIS IS YOUR LIBRARY

Treat this book as you would treat your own, so that others may benefit from and enjoy it's use.

This book is to be returned on or before the due date stamped on the back. If it is wanted for a further period, it may be renewed by phone.

Book damages and losses shall be made good by the borrower by replacement or payment of the book's value.

For late returns, a fine of 2¢ per book per day will be imposed.

Base Library Officer

The Short Tree and the Bird That Could Not Sing

Written by
Dennis Foon

Pictures by
John Bianchi

A Groundwood Book
Douglas & McIntyre
VANCOUVER/TORONTO

For Rebecca

D.F.

For Jessica and Sascha

J.B.

Text copyright © 1986 by Dennis Foon
Illustrations copyright © 1986 by John Bianchi

Douglas & McIntyre Ltd., 1615 Venables Street,
Vancouver, British Columbia V5L 2H1

Canadian Cataloguing in Publication Data

Foon, Dennis, 1951–
    The short tree and the bird that could not sing

ISBN 0-88899-046-4

I. Bianchi, John.   II. Title.

PS8561.066S54 1986   jC813'.54   C86-094042-X
PZ7.F65Sh 1986

Designed by Michael Solomon
Printed and bound in Hong Kong

ONCE upon a time there was a very short, very sad tree.

Some trees grow tall so they can see quite far away.
They watch dogs biting postmen and car crash derbies
and firemen squirting each other with hoses and many,
many other things.

But the short tree could only see the crooked brook that bubbled by his roots. Though the tree thought the brook was pleasant, he was tired of counting bubbles day after day. The tree became sadder and sadder and sadder.

One day he heard an awful noise.

"Ow-ow-ow-ouch!" yowled the tree. "What a horrendous racket!"

"That is not a racket," said a voice. "That is my song. I am singing *On Top of Spaghetti.*"

"You are singing out of tune," said the tree. "Plus you have the words all wrong."

The tree noticed that a bird had landed on him.

"If I stopped singing, would you mind if I rested on your branch for a little while?" asked the bird.

"Not one bit," replied the tree. "As long as you do not sing."

"It's a deal," sighed the bird. "Did you know you have excellent branches?"

"Pardon me?" asked the tree.

"Most tree branches are far too thick for me to hold onto. Yours are just the right size."

"Pshaw," said the tree, blushing beneath his bark. "Really?"

"I mean it. I like your branches," the bird repeated. "But I don't know if I like you. I haven't known you long enough."

"Oh," peeped the tree.

"But I do think it is safe to say that I will soon grow to like you and we shall become friends," said the bird.

"Oh, good!" exclaimed the tree.

And the bird was right. They did become friends.

Every day the bird flew into the sky and came back to tell the tree what she had seen.

One day she visited a cloud where a family of escaped balloons was hiding.

Another time she flew to the top of a mountain to be the witness at a snow people's wedding.

Once the bird reported on a circus that was in town.

The bird brought the tree a fluffy pink piece of cotton candy from the midway.

"That is kind of you," said the tree, "but I don't eat candy."

"That's all right. Neither do I," answered the bird. "But I do like the colour, don't you?"

"I think it's charming. Pink is one of my favourite colours," said the tree.

So the bird decorated the tree with pink cotton candy. When it rained, all the cotton candy melted from the tree's branches and went into the ground. This made the ants happy, because ants love cotton candy.

After the rain, the air became chilly. Fall was on its way.

One day the bird came to the tree and said, "I have to go away."

"Good," said the tree. "You can tell me all about it this afternoon when you return."

"I won't be back this afternoon," said the bird. "I will be gone all fall and winter. I am flying south where it is warm and there are tourists on the beaches and coconuts on the trees."

"Don't go," pleaded the tree. "If you stay, I'll grow coconuts and find you some tourists and beaches."

"First of all, you cannot grow coconuts, and if you did they would be quite small and not very tasty," said the bird. "Also, there will soon be snow all around you, and people do not like to lie in the snow when they are wearing their bathing suits. And most of all, I am a bird and if I do not go south I will catch a cold and get terrible sneezes and probably die. I like you very much and I do not want to die because then I would not see you again. On the other hand, if I do go south, I will come back and see you in the spring."

"But I can keep you warm, Bird. You can nest in my branches and stay warm in my leaves. Please stay!" begged the tree.

"No," replied the bird. "I have to go."

"But I'll miss you!" cried the tree.

"When the wind whistles through your branches, think of my song."

"But your song is horrible," shuddered the tree.

"Well," said the bird, "in any case, I have to go now. Goodbye."

"Goodbye," said the very sad and very short tree.

For a long time the tree was angry at the bird.

"It's easy for her to go," thought the tree. "She has wings. She can fly where she wants. I have roots and I'm stuck in the ground. I can't seem to grow coconuts. And I haven't seen even one tourist, no sand at all and not a drop of suntan lotion." Then the tree cried as he watched his leaves fall off one by one. "Oh, Bird," cried the tree. "I wish you were here."

But the bird was in Florida eating Coney Island hot dogs and taking long swims in the ocean.

"Oh, Bird," wept the sad, sad tree. "Come back and tell me what you see."

Soon winter came and the wind was cold. The crooked brook froze and its bubbles went to sleep in the ice. The tree was chilled down to his roots.

"It is rather lucky that Bird is not here now. This cold wind would go right through her feathers and give her terrible deadly sneezes," thought the tree.

Just then the wind began to whistle through his branches. And the whistling sounded familiar.

"Ow-ow-ow-ouch!" cried the tree. "The wind sounds just like Bird singing *On Top of Spaghetti.*"

But the tree smiled underneath his bark because he liked to think about his friend.

One morning the tree felt the sun warming his branches and trunk. And the grass at his roots was starting to nudge its way up through the brown moss.

The ice in the crooked brook started to crack and float away. And the bubbles woke up and were everywhere, dancing so fast the tree kept losing count of them.

Just then the tree heard the sound the wind made when it whistled through his branches. "Oh, my aching head," moaned the tree. "The wind is whistling *On Top of Spaghetti* again, only this time it sounds even worse!"

And then the tree thought, "But there is no wind right now. I don't feel any wind blowing through my branches."

It was the bird.

"Hello, Tree," said the bird. "I'm back."

"Hello, Bird," said the tree. "Welcome."

"I've brought you a piece of beach ball to wear," said the bird, "because you look so good in pink."

"Thank you very much," said the tree.

And the bird tied the shred of pink beach ball to the
tree's littlest branch. And then the bird sang, and the tree
groaned, and the brook bubbled, and the spring was
warm, and wet, and green.

THE END

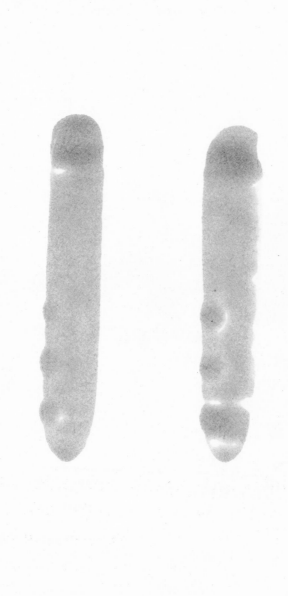

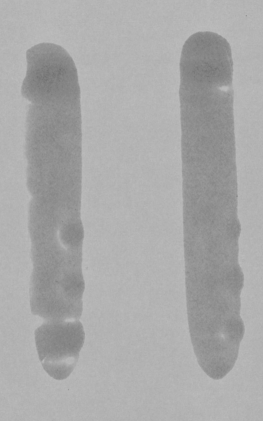